Now Hiring . . .

Sarah went on down the street. And there on the corner she saw the sign. It wasn't very big, and it was stuck to a folding door. It said "Help Wanted."

The folding door was at one end of a shoeshine stand. The stand was a kind of shed with a platform on it. There were four chairs on the platform. Above the chairs was a big sign: "Al's Shoeshine Corner."

A man sat on one of the chairs. He put down his newspaper and slid down off the chair. His shoulders were stooped. He wasn't much taller than she was. "You want something?" he asked.

"I'm Sarah Ida Becker," she said, "and I want to work for you."

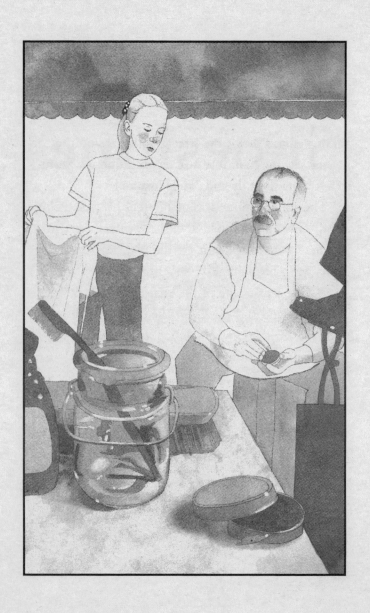

CLYDE ROBERT BULLA

Shoeshine Girl

Illustrated by
JIM BURKE

HarperTrophy®
An Imprint of HarperCollins*Publishers*

Harper Trophy® is a registered trademark
of HarperCollins Publishers Inc.

Shoeshine Girl

Text copyright © 1975 by Clyde Robert Bulla

Illustrations copyright © 2000 by Jim Burke

Library of Congress Cataloging-in-Publication Data

Bulla, Clyde Robert.

 Shoeshine girl / Clyde Robert Bulla ; illustrated by Jim Burke.

  p.   cm.

 Newly illustrated ed.

 Summary: Determined to earn some money, ten-year-old Sarah
Ida gets a job at a shoeshine stand and learns a great many things
besides shining shoes.

 ISBN 0-690-04830-0 (lib. bdg.) — ISBN 0-06-440228-2 (pbk.)

 [1. Friendship—Fiction. 2. Behavior—Fiction. 3. Shoe
shiners—Fiction.] I. Burke, Jim, ill. II. Title.

PZ7.B912Sh 2000   99-2006

[Fic]—dc21   CIP

First Harper Trophy edition, 1989

Newly illustrated Harper Trophy edition, 2000

Revised Harper Trophy edition, 2004

Visit us on the World Wide Web!

www.harperchildrens.com

16 17 18 19 20 OPM 60 59 58 57 56 55

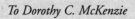
To Dorothy C. McKenzie

CONTENTS

Shoeshine Girl

Palmville

The train stopped at Palmville, and Sarah Ida had a sudden thought. What if she didn't get off? What if she just rode on to the end of the line? Maybe she could find a place where everything was new and she could start all over again.

But people would ask questions. *How old are you? . . . Only ten and a half? What are you doing here all by yourself?* Someone would be sure to find her and bring her back.

Anyway, it was too late. Aunt Claudia had already seen her. Aunt Claudia was at the station, looking through the train window and waving.

1

Sarah Ida picked up her suitcase.

"Here, little lady, I'll help you with that," said the porter.

"I can carry it myself," she said, and she dragged it off the train.

Aunt Claudia gave her a kiss that smelled like cough drops. Then they took a taxi. They rode through town, and Aunt Claudia talked. "You've grown, but I knew you the minute I saw you. You've got your mother's pretty brown eyes, but you've got your father's jaw. Look—over there. That's our new super-market. Things may seem quiet to you here, after the city, but I think you'll like Palmville. It's getting to be quite a city, too."

Sarah Ida said nothing.

"We're on Grand Avenue," said Aunt Claudia. "It's the main street." The taxi turned off the avenue and stopped in front of a square, gray house.

While Aunt Claudia paid the driver, Sarah Ida looked at the house. It was old, with a new coat of paint. It had spidery-looking porches and balconies.

2

They went inside.

"There's the telephone," said Aunt Claudia. "Your mother wanted you to call as soon as you got here."

"Why?" asked Sarah Ida.

"So she'd know you got here all right."

"*You* call her," said Sarah Ida.

"All right." Aunt Claudia went to the telephone. "I'll dial the number for you."

"Don't dial it for me," said Sarah Ida. "I'm not going to talk to her."

Aunt Claudia's mouth opened and closed. Then she said, "It's been a long trip, and I know you're tired. Come on upstairs. Shall I help you with your suitcase?"

"No," said Sarah Ida.

They climbed the stairs. Aunt Claudia opened a door. "This is your room."

Sarah Ida looked about the room. It wasn't bad. She rather liked the rag rugs on the dark wood floor, and she didn't mind the rocking chair. But the window curtains were fussy. So was the bed cover. And the pictures on the

4

wall were terrible—a fat girl looking at a robin, and a horse with a blue ribbon around its neck.

She waited for Aunt Claudia to ask, "How do you like it?" She was going to answer, "I like *plain* things."

But Aunt Claudia didn't ask. "Maybe you want to unpack now," she said. "We can talk later."

"We can talk now if you want to." Sarah Ida sat down on the bed.

Aunt Claudia sat in the rocking chair.

"We don't have to pretend," said Sarah Ida.

Aunt Claudia looked puzzled. "Pretend?"

"About anything. You don't have to pretend you want me here—"

"I do want you here!" said Aunt Claudia.

"I doubt that. I doubt it very much." Sarah Ida kept her voice cool. "I certainly didn't want to come. And I wouldn't be here if my father and mother hadn't wanted to get rid of me for the summer."

"We're not off to a very good start, are we?"

5

Aunt Claudia smiled a little. "Here's the way I understand it. Your father's work takes him away from home a lot. You and your mother have had a few problems. Your mother isn't well—"

"That's what she says," said Sarah Ida.

"Your mother isn't well," Aunt Claudia said again, "and you weren't making things easy for her. She and your father thought it would be better if you came here for a while."

"That's their story," said Sarah Ida.

"Do you want to tell yours?"

"Not especially. I don't think you'd listen."

"You could try and see."

"Well—" Sarah Ida began. "For a long time nobody cared what I did. Nobody paid any attention. Then all at once everything changed. Mother asked a million questions about everything I did. And my clothes weren't right, and my friends weren't right. I couldn't do this—I couldn't do that."

"You say everything changed all at once," said Aunt Claudia. "Why was that?"

Sarah Ida looked away.

"You had a friend named Midge, didn't you?" said Aunt Claudia. "And Midge got into trouble. The way I heard it, she was taking a dress out of a store. It was a dress she hadn't paid for."

"She wasn't stealing," said Sarah Ida.

"What do you call it?" asked Aunt Claudia.

"She was just trying to see if she could get it out of the store. It was like—it was like a game. Anyway, what does it have to do with me?"

"Maybe nothing," said Aunt Claudia. "But she was a good friend of yours. If you'd been with her when she took the dress, you might have been in trouble, too. Maybe that's why your father and mother started to worry about you."

"They started to worry about me because they don't trust me," said Sarah Ida.

Aunt Claudia asked, "Do you always give them reason to trust you?"

"It's easy to see whose side you're on," said Sarah Ida.

Aunt Claudia stood up. "I'd better start

7

dinner. Put your things away if you want to. Or you can rest a while."

She went downstairs.

Sarah Ida put her feet on the bed. She was *tired*. But if she lay here alone in this strange room, she might start crying. And crying wouldn't help.

She got up. She opened her suitcase and began to unpack.

Rossi

In the morning Sarah Ida put on an old shirt and her oldest blue jeans. She went down into the kitchen.

Aunt Claudia was there, frying bacon and eggs. "Good morning," she said. "Did you sleep well?"

"Yes," said Sarah Ida.

"There's apple jelly and plum jam. Which would you like with your toast?"

"Neither one."

They sat down to breakfast. Aunt Claudia said, "You're going to have company."

"Who?" asked Sarah Ida.

"Rossi Wigginhorn."

Sarah Ida frowned. "I don't know any Rossi Wigginhorn."

"She's a neighbor," said Aunt Claudia. "She's been wanting to meet you."

"Why?"

"I told her you were coming. I thought it would be nice if you had a friend your own age."

"Did you ever think," said Sarah Ida, "that I might like to choose my friends?"

"I like to choose my friends, too," said Aunt Claudia. "But when you're in a new place and haven't had a chance to meet anybody —"

"It doesn't matter," said Sarah Ida, "whether I meet anybody or not."

They finished breakfast.

Aunt Claudia asked, "Can you cook?"

"No," said Sarah Ida.

"Would you like to learn?"

"No."

"At least, you'd better learn to make your own breakfast," said Aunt Claudia. "It's something you might need to know. And there are

10

things you can do to help me. I'll teach you to take care of your room, and you can help me with the cleaning and dusting."

"How much do you pay?" asked Sarah Ida.

Aunt Claudia stared at her. "Pay?"

"Money," said Sarah Ida. "How much money?"

Aunt Claudia took the dishes to the sink. She came back to the table and sat down. "I don't like to bring this up," she said, "but I suppose I must. I'm not supposed to pay you anything."

"And why not?" asked Sarah Ida.

"Because your mother asked me not to. She told me you had borrowed your allowance for the next two months. She said you had spent it all and had nothing to show for it. She asked me not to give you any money while you're here."

"But I've *got* to have money!" said Sarah Ida. "I'm going to *need* it!"

"What for?" asked Aunt Claudia.

"Lots of things. Candy and gum. Movies —

11

and popcorn when I go to the movies. I need it for magazines. And for clothes."

"If you need clothes, I'll buy them," said Aunt Claudia. "We can talk later about movies. If I buy you a ticket once a week—"

"I want money in my pocket!"

Aunt Claudia sighed. "That seems to be what your mother *doesn't* want. I think she's trying to teach you the value of money."

"I *know* the value of money, and if you think you can—!"

"All right, Sarah Ida. That's enough."

Sarah Ida ran up to her room. She could feel herself shaking. They didn't know how she felt about money. They didn't understand, and she didn't know how to tell them. She *needed* money in her pocket. It didn't have to be much. But she just didn't feel *right* with none at all!

Aunt Claudia was calling her.

Sarah Ida didn't answer.

"Sarah Ida!" Aunt Claudia called again. "Rossi is here."

Sarah Ida lay on the bed and looked out the window.

"Rossi has something for you," said Aunt Claudia. "Is it all right if she brings it up?"

"No!" said Sarah Ida. She went downstairs.

Rossi was waiting in the hall. She had pink cheeks and pale yellow hair. She wore a yellow dress without a spot or a wrinkle.

"I brought some cupcakes," she said. "I made them myself."

"That was sweet of you, Rossi," said Aunt Claudia.

"Yes, that was sweet of you, Rossi," said Sarah Ida.

Aunt Claudia gave her a sharp look. Then she left them alone.

The girls sat on the porch. They each ate a cupcake.

"I think you're awfully brave, coming here all by yourself," said Rossi.

"It was no big thing," said Sarah Ida. "My father put me on the train, and my aunt was here to meet me."

"Well, it's a long trip. I'd have been scared. Are you having a good time in Palmville?"

"I just got here," said Sarah Ida.

"I think you'll like it. There's a lot to see. Come on down the street. I'll show you where I live."

They walked down to Rossi's house. It was old, like Aunt Claudia's. It was half covered with creepy-looking vines.

Sarah Ida met Rossi's mother. Mrs. Wigginhorn was pretty in the same way Rossi was. She had pale hair and a sweet smile.

She said, "I hope you'll enjoy your visit here."

Rossi showed Sarah Ida her room. "My daddy made this shelf for my library. These are all my books. Any time you want to borrow some—"

"I don't read much," said Sarah Ida. She was looking at something else. She was looking at a blue and white pig on the dresser. "What's this?" she asked.

"That's my bank," said Rossi.

"Is there anything in it?"

"About five dollars."

Sarah Ida picked up the pig. It was heavy. She turned it from side to side. She could feel the coins move.

"I need four dollars," she said. "Will you lend it to me?"

"I — I'm saving for a present for my daddy," said Rossi.

"It's just a loan. I'll pay you back."

Rossi looked unhappy. "I'm not supposed to lend money."

"You said I could borrow your books. What's the difference?"

"I just don't think I'd better."

"All right. Forget it." Sarah Ida went to the door.

"No. Wait. You can have it." Rossi was feeling in the top drawer of the dresser. She took out a tiny key on a string. "But don't tell anyone."

"Don't you tell, either," said Sarah Ida.

There was a lock on the underside of the

16

pig. Rossi unlocked it. The coins fell out on the dresser. They were mostly quarters and dimes.

Sarah Ida counted out four dollars. "Are you sure you want to do this?"

"Yes," said Rossi.

"Well, then, good-by," said Sarah Ida.

"Don't you want me to walk back with you?" asked Rossi.

"You don't need to." Sarah Ida left her. She walked out of the house and up the street. The coins jingled in her pocket. She was whistling when she got back to Aunt Claudia's.

A Game?

She awoke late the next morning. There was sunlight in the room. She looked at the pictures on the walls. For the first time she almost liked them. For the first time in weeks she felt almost happy.

The feeling was quickly gone.

The door opened, and Aunt Claudia came in. Her face was like winter.

She said, "You took money from Rossi yesterday—didn't you?"

Sarah Ida sat up in bed. "How—?"

"Mrs. Wigginhorn called me. She said most of the money was gone from Rossi's bank. She said you would know about it."

18

A Game?

"I didn't—" began Sarah Ida.

"What happened? I want to know."

"I borrowed the money. That's what happened. I *borrowed* it."

"You hadn't known poor little Rossi even a day, and already you were borrowing her money."

"Poor little Rossi said I could."

"She's such a friendly child. She didn't know how to say no." Aunt Claudia asked, "Is money so important to you? What do you need it for?"

"I told you. I like to have money in my pocket."

"Do you think that's a good reason?"

"It is to me."

"It isn't to me. Get your clothes on and take that money right back."

Sarah Ida hadn't known Aunt Claudia could sound so fierce. She got up and dressed. The money was in an envelope under her pillow. She stuffed it into her pocket.

She went down the street to the Wigginhorns'. Rossi opened the door. Her eyes and nose were red.

"Sarah Ida—"

"Here." Sarah Ida almost threw the envelope at her. "I might have known I couldn't trust you."

"I couldn't help it," said Rossi. "Mother saw the key on the dresser. She picked up the bank and found out it was almost empty. She kept asking questions till I had to tell her."

"Just forget it," said Sarah Ida coldly. "Forget the whole thing."

She walked away.

Back at Aunt Claudia's, she started up to her room. Aunt Claudia called her. "Your breakfast is ready."

"I don't want any," said Sarah Ida.

"Come here, anyway," said Aunt Claudia. Sarah Ida stood in the kitchen doorway.

"I shouldn't have lost my temper," said Aunt Claudia, "but you don't seem to understand that what you did was wrong."

"I don't see why it was wrong," said Sarah Ida.

"It's wrong to take advantage of someone. And you took advantage of Rossi."

"If you'd let me have some money, I wouldn't have had to borrow."

Aunt Claudia's lips closed tightly for a moment. She said, "This is a game, isn't it?"

"A game?"

"You're trying me out, to see how far you can go."

"I don't know what you mean."

"I think you do. Money really isn't that important to you, is it? You're just using this whole thing to get what you want. At the same time, you're trying to strike back at me, because—"

"The money *is* important!" cried Sarah Ida. "And if you won't give me any, I'll—I'll go out and get some!"

"How?" asked Aunt Claudia.

"I'll get a job."

"Where?"

"I don't know, but I'll find one. But if I did, you wouldn't let me keep it. You want to keep me under your thumb."

A Game?

"Sarah Ida, stop this!" said Aunt Claudia. "If you could find work and earn some money, I wouldn't keep you from it. But ask yourself—what could you do? Who would give you a job? I don't want you under my thumb. All I'm trying to do is—"

"I *know* what you're trying to do. And if you think I'm playing a game, I'll show you!"

She rushed out of the house. Aunt Claudia's voice followed her. "Come back! Stop!"

Sarah Ida didn't stop. She cut across the yard and ran up the street.

On the Avenue

She came to Grand Avenue. She was out of breath, and there was a pounding in her ears.

She stopped in the doorway of a drugstore and looked up and down the street. People were walking by. Cars were passing. Palmville was bigger than she'd thought. In all these stores there must be someone who would give her some work to do.

There was a dress shop across the street, with girls' dresses in the window. She might try there. But she wasn't even wearing a dress, and she didn't look very neat.

She used the drugstore window as a mirror

and tried to comb her hair with her fingers. Inside the store a woman was watching her. She looked friendly. Sarah Ida went in.

"Can I help you?" asked the woman.

"I—" Sarah Ida began, and she couldn't go on. How could she say "I want to work for you"? What kind of work could she do in a drugstore?

"Yes?" said the woman.

"I'm just looking," said Sarah Ida. She looked at the candy, but she couldn't say, "I'll have this and this," because she didn't have any money.

She went outside. She walked past a restaurant, a bank, a hardware store. She came to a pet shop. There were puppies in one window and kittens in the other. She put out her hand to the puppies. One of them came to the window and put his nose against the glass.

She went into the shop. A man and woman were there. All about the shop were animals in cages. There were birds, and in one cage was a green and yellow parrot.

"Do you need help here?" asked Sarah Ida.

The parrot began to squawk. "Polly, Polly! Pretty Polly! My, oh my!"

"What?" asked the woman.

"I said, do you need help!" shouted Sarah Ida.

"Be quiet!" said the woman. "Not you, little girl. I mean that silly bird."

"Silly bird!" said the parrot. "My, oh my!"

The woman threw a cloth over the cage, and the parrot was quiet.

"Now. What was it you wanted?" she asked.

"I wanted to work for you," said Sarah Ida.

"Oh," said the woman.

The man spoke. "What do you know about animals?"

"Not much, but I could learn."

The man said, "Come back when you're a little older."

"How much older?"

"About six years," said the man.

"Do you know where I *could* get work?" she asked.

"What can you do?"

26

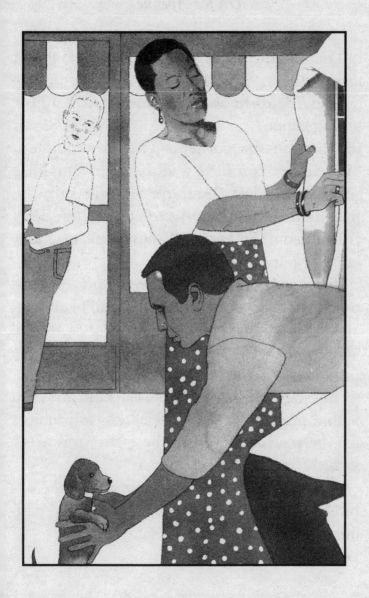

"I—I don't know."

"You might try Al," said the man. "He's got a sign up."

"Yes," said the woman. "He's had it up for a long time."

"He's on the corner." The man pointed. "Why don't you have a look?"

Sarah Ida left the shop. She was sure the man and woman had just been trying to get rid of her. She thought they were probably laughing at her, too.

She went on down the street. And there on the corner she saw the sign. It wasn't very big, and it was stuck to a folding door. It said "Help Wanted."

The folding door was at one end of a shoeshine stand. The stand was a kind of shed with a platform in it. There were four chairs on the platform. Above the chairs was a big sign: "Al's Shoeshine Corner."

A man sat on one of the chairs. His face was hidden behind the newspaper he was reading.

Sarah Ida looked at the "Help Wanted" sign. She looked at the stand. This was the place, she thought. This was just the place!

She would tell Aunt Claudia, "I have a job."

"What kind?" Aunt Claudia would ask.

"Working at a shoeshine stand," Sarah Ida would say. "A shoeshine stand on Grand Avenue."

"Oh, you can't do that!" Aunt Claudia would say.

"You said you wouldn't keep me from earning some money," Sarah Ida would say.

"But you can't be seen working at a shoeshine stand on Grand Avenue," Aunt Claudia would say. "I'll *give* you some money!"

Sarah Ida spoke to the man. "Are you Al?"

He put down the newspaper, and she saw his face. He was not young. His hair was thin and gray. His eyes looked like little pieces of coal set far back in his head.

"Yes, I'm Al." He slid down off the chair. His shoulders were stooped. He wasn't much taller than she was. "You want something?"

29

"I'm Sarah Ida Becker," she said, "and I want to work for you."

"What do you mean, work for me?"

"Your sign says 'Help Wanted.'"

"I put that up so long ago I forgot about it," he said. "Nobody wants to work for me. People don't like to get their hands dirty. They want to do something easy that pays big money."

"Will you give me a job?" she asked.

"You're not a boy."

"The sign doesn't say you wanted a boy."

A man came by.

"Shine?" asked Al.

The man climbed into a chair. Al shined his shoes. The man went on.

Al looked at Sarah Ida. "You still here?"

"If I worked for you, what would I have to do?" she asked.

"Shine shoes, same as I do. Some days I get more work than I can take care of. Then I need help. But whoever heard of a shoe-shine girl?"

30

"Why couldn't a girl shine shoes?"

"Why don't you go on home?"

"You said you needed help. You've got your sign up."

"What do you want to work here for?"

"I need some money."

"You wouldn't get rich here."

"I know that."

He looked her up and down. "I don't think you really want to work."

All at once she was tired of waiting, tired of talking. She started away.

Al said, "What did you say your name was? Sarah what?"

"Sarah Ida Becker."

"You any relation to the lady that used to be in the library? You any relation to Miss Claudia Becker?"

"She's my aunt."

Another man stopped for a shoeshine. When he was gone, Al asked her, "You staying with your aunt?"

"Yes," she said.

31

"Go tell her you saw Al Winkler. Tell her you want to work for me. Maybe —"

"Maybe what?"

"I don't know yet," he said. "First you see what she says."

The Shoeshine Man

Aunt Claudia was waiting on the porch. "Sit down," she said, when Sarah Ida came up the steps. "I want to talk to you."

Sarah Ida sat in the porch swing.

"You must never do this again," said Aunt Claudia. "You must always let me know where you're going. Do you understand?"

"Yes," said Sarah Ida.

"Where have you been?"

"On the avenue."

"What were you doing?"

"Looking for a job. And I found one."

"You found one?"

"Yes, I did."

"Where?"

"On Grand Avenue. Working for the shoe-shine man."

"*Who?*"

"Al Winkler, the shoeshine man."

Aunt Claudia looked dazed. "How did you know him?"

"I didn't know him. He had a 'Help Wanted' sign and I stopped."

"Al Winkler," said Aunt Claudia, as if she were talking to herself. "I remember him so well. He came to the library when I worked there. He hadn't gone to school much, and he wanted to learn more. I helped him choose books." She asked, "Does he want you to work at his stand?"

"He said to talk to you about it."

"Do you want to work for him?" asked Aunt Claudia.

"I told you, I want some money of my own."

"This might be a good way to earn some," said Aunt Claudia.

"You *want* me to shine shoes on Grand Avenue?"

"If that's what you want to do."

Sarah Ida was quiet for a while. Things weren't working out the way she'd planned. She'd never thought Aunt Claudia would let her work in the shoeshine stand, and Aunt Claudia didn't seem to care!

Unless— Sarah Ida had another thought. Maybe Aunt Claudia didn't believe she'd go through with it. Maybe she was thinking, *That child is playing another game.*

Sarah Ida said, "You really want me to go tell Al Winkler I'll work for him?"

"If it's what you want to do," said Aunt Claudia.

Sarah Ida started down the steps. Aunt Claudia didn't call her back. There was nothing for her to do but go.

*   *   *

She found Al sitting in one of his chairs.

"What did she say?" he asked.

"She said yes."

35

"You want to start now?"

"I don't care," she said.

He opened a drawer under the platform and took out an old piece of cloth. "Use this for an apron. Tie it around you."

She tied it around her waist.

A man stopped at the stand. He was a big man with a round face and a black beard. He climbed into a chair and put his feet on the shoe rests.

"How are you, Mr. Naylor?" said Al.

"Not bad," said the man. "Who's the young lady?"

"She's helping me," said Al. "She needs practice. You mind if she practices on you?"

"I don't mind," said Mr. Naylor.

Al said to Sarah Ida, "I'm going to shine one shoe. You watch what I do. Then you shine the other one."

He took two soft brushes and brushed the man's shoe.

"That takes off the dust," he said. "Always start with a clean shoe."

36

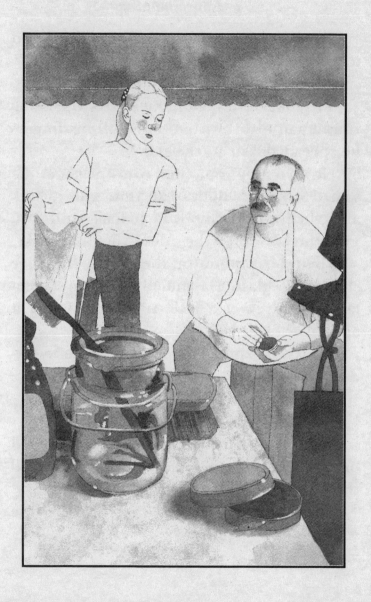

He picked up a jar of water with an old toothbrush in it. With the toothbrush he sprinkled a few drops of water on the shoe.

"That makes a better shine." He opened a round can of brown polish. With his fingers he spread polish on the shoe.

"Now you lay your cloth over the shoe," he said. "Stretch it tight—like this. Pull it back and forth—like this. Rub it hard and fast. First the toe—then the sides—then the back."

When he put down the cloth, the shoe shone like glass. He untied the man's shoelace. He drew it a little tighter and tied it again.

He asked Sarah Ida, "Did you see everything I did?"

"Yes," she said.

"All right. Let's see you do it."

She picked up the brushes. She dropped one. When she bent to pick it up, she dropped the other one. Her face grew hot.

She brushed the shoe. She sprinkled the water.

"Not so much," Al told her. "You don't need much."

She looked at the brown polish. "Do I have to get this on my fingers?"

"You can put it on with a rag, but it's not the best way. You can rub it in better with your fingers."

"I don't want to get it on my hands."

"Your hands will wash."

She put the polish on with her fingers. She shined Mr. Naylor's shoe. She untied his shoelace, pulled it tight, and tried to tie it again.

Al tied it for her. "It's hard to tie someone else's shoe when you never did it before."

Mr. Naylor looked at his shoes. "Best shine I've had all year," he said. He paid Al. He gave Sarah Ida a dollar bill.

After he had gone, she asked Al, "Why did he give me this?"

"That's your tip," said Al. "You didn't earn it. He gave it to you because you're just getting started."

"Will everybody give me a dollar?" she asked.

"No," he said, "and don't be looking for it."

Others stopped at the stand. Sometimes two or three were there at once. Part of the time Sarah Ida put polish on shoes. Part of the time she used the polishing cloth.

Toward the end of the day she grew tired. She tried to hurry. That was when she put black polish on a man's brown shoe.

The man began to shout. "Look what you did!"

"It's not hurt," said Al. "I can take the black polish off. Sarah Ida, hand me the jar of water."

She reached for the jar and knocked it over. All the water ran out.

"Go around the corner to the filling station," Al told her. "There's a drinking fountain outside. Fill the jar and bring it back."

Sarah Ida brought the water. Al washed the man's shoe. All the black polish came off.

"See?" he said. "It's as good as new."

"Well, maybe," said the man, "but I don't want *her* giving me any more shines."

He went away.

Sarah Ida made a face. "He was mean."

"No, he wasn't," said Al. "He just didn't want black polish on his brown shoes."

"Anyone can make a mistake," she said.

"That's right. Just don't make too many." He said, "You can go now." He gave her a dollar. "This is to go with your other dollar."

"Is that all the pay I get?"

"You'll get more when you're worth more," he said. "You can come back tomorrow afternoon. That's my busy time. Come about one."

She didn't answer. She turned her back on him and walked away.

The
Boy on the Street

In the morning she told Aunt Claudia, "I'm going to the drugstore."

"Aren't you working for Al?" asked Aunt Claudia.

"Maybe I am, and maybe I'm not," said Sarah Ida.

In the drugstore she looked at magazines. She looked at chewing gum and candy bars. None of them seemed to matter much. Her money was the first she had ever worked for. Somehow she wanted to spend it for something important.

She went home with the two dollars still in her pocket.

She and Aunt Claudia had lunch.

"If you aren't working for Al," said Aunt Claudia, "you can help me."

"I'm going to work," said Sarah Ida. Working for Al was certainly better than helping Aunt Claudia.

She went down to the shoeshine stand.

"So you came back," said Al.

"Yes," she said.

"I didn't know if you would or not."

Customers were coming. Al told Sarah Ida what to do. Once she shined a pair of shoes all by herself.

They were busy most of the afternoon. Her hair fell down into her eyes. Her back hurt from bending over.

Late in the day Al told her, "You've had enough for now. You can go. You got some tips, didn't you?"

"Yes," she said. "Do you want me to count them?"

"No. You can keep them. And here's your pay." He gave her two dollars. "And I want to tell you something. When you get through with a customer, you say 'thank you.' "

"All right," she said.

"One more thing. You didn't say yesterday if you were coming back or not. This time I want to know. Are you coming back tomorrow?"

"Yes," she said.

"Come about the same time," he said. "I'm going to bring you something."

* * *

What he brought her was a white canvas apron. It had two pockets. It had straps that went over her shoulders and tied in the back. There were black letters across the front.

"Why does it say 'Lane's Lumber Company'?" she asked. "Why doesn't it say 'Al's Shoeshine Corner'?"

"Because it came from Lane's Lumber Company," he said. "Fred Lane is a friend of mine, and he gave it to me."

It was nothing but a canvas apron. She didn't know why she should be so pleased with it. But it was a long time since anything had pleased her as much. She liked the stiff, new feel of the cloth. The pockets were deep. She liked to put her hands into them.

That night she thought about the apron. She had left it locked up at the stand. She almost told her mother and father about it in the letter she wrote them. She had promised to write twice a week — to make Aunt Claudia happy. But she didn't think they would care about her apron. All she wrote was:

> Dear Mother and Father,
>   I am all right. Everything is all right here. It was hot today.
>
> > Good-by,
> > SARAH IDA

She didn't tell Aunt Claudia about her apron. She didn't feel too friendly toward Aunt Claudia.

There were times when she didn't even feel too friendly toward Al.

There was the time when she shined an old man's shoes. He paid her and went away.

Al said, "I didn't hear you say 'thank you.' "

"He didn't give me any tip," she said. "The old stingy-guts."

They were alone at the stand. Al said, "What did you call him?"

"Old stingy-guts," she said. "That's what he is."

"Don't you ever say a thing like that again," said Al in a cold, hard voice. "He didn't have to give you a tip. Nobody has to. If he wants to give you something extra, that's his business. But if he doesn't, that's his business, too. I want to hear you say 'thank you' whether you get any tip or not."

It scared her a little to see him so angry. She didn't speak to him for quite a while.

But that evening he said, as if nothing had happened, "I could use some help in the morning, too. You want to work here all day?"

"I don't know," she said.

"You can if you want to. Ask your aunt."

She started home. On the way, a boy caught

up with her. His arms and legs were long, and he took long steps. He looked ugly, with his lower lip pushed out. He asked, "What are you doing working for Al?"

She walked faster. He kept up with her. "How much is he paying you?"

"I don't see why I should tell you," she said.

"You've got my job, that's why."

The light turned green, and she crossed the street. He didn't follow her.

All evening she thought about what the boy had said. In the morning she asked Al about it.

"Was he a skinny boy?" asked Al. "Did he have light hair?"

"Yes," she said.

"That was Kicker."

"His name is *Kicker?*"

"That's what he called himself when he was little. Now we all call him that. He's my neighbor."

"What did he mean when he said I had his job?"

48

"I don't know. Once I asked him if he wanted to work for me. He said he did. Then he never came to work. He didn't want the job, but I guess he doesn't want you to have it, either."

"Maybe he changed his mind," she said. "Maybe he wants to work for you now."

"Maybe," said Al. "I'll have a talk with him. I don't think you'll see him any more."

But later in the week she did see him. He was across the street, watching her.

The Medal

Every evening, after work, Sarah Ida was tired. But every morning she was ready to go back to Shoeshine Corner. It wasn't that she liked shining shoes, but things *happened* at the shoeshine stand. Every customer was different. Every day she found out something new.

Some things she learned by herself. Like how much polish to use on a shoe. A thin coat gave a better and quicker shine. Some things Al told her. "When a customer comes here, he gets more than a shine," he said. "He gets to rest in a chair. When you rub with the cloth, it feels good on his feet. When you tie his shoelaces a little tighter, it makes his shoes fit better. My customers go away feeling a little better. Anyway, I *hope* they do."

One warm, cloudy afternoon, he said, "We might as well close up."

"Why?" she asked. "It's only three o'clock."

"It's going to rain. Nobody gets a shine on a rainy day."

He began to put away the brushes and shoe polish. She helped him.

"Maybe you can run home before the rain," he said. A few big drops splashed on the sidewalk. "No. Too late now."

They sat under the little roof, out of the rain.

"Hear that sound?" he said. "Every time I hear rain on a tin roof, I get to thinking about when I was a boy. We lived in an old truck with a tin roof over the back."

"You *lived* in a truck?"

"Most of the time. We slept under the tin roof, and when it rained, the sound put me to sleep. We went all over the South in that truck."

"You and your mother and father?"

"My dad and I."

"What were you doing, driving all over the South?"

"My dad sold medicine."

"What kind?"

"Something to make you strong and keep you from getting sick."

"Did you take it?"

"No. I guess it wasn't any good."

She had never heard him talk much about himself before. She wanted him to go on.

"Was it fun living in a truck?"

"Fun? I wouldn't say so. Riding along was all right. Sometimes my dad and I stopped close to the woods, and that was all right, too. But I never liked it when we were in town selling medicine. Dad would play the mouth harp, and he made me sing. He wanted me to dance a jig, too, but I never could."

She tried to imagine Al as a little boy. She couldn't at all. "Why did he want you to sing and dance?" she asked.

"To draw a crowd. When there was a crowd, he sold medicine. We didn't stay anywhere very long. Except once. We stayed in one place six months. My dad did farm work, and I went to school."

He told her about the school. It was just outside a town. The teacher was Miss Miller. The schoolhouse had only one room.

"There was this big stove," he said, "and that winter I kept the fire going. Miss Miller never had to carry coal when I was there."

"Did you like her?" asked Sarah Ida. "Was she a good teacher?"

"Best teacher I ever had. Of course, she was just about the *only* one. I hadn't been to school much, but she took time to show me things. Do teachers still give medals in school?"

"Sometimes. Not very often."

"Miss Miller gave medals. They were all alike. Every one had a star on it. At the end of school you got one if you were the best in reading or spelling or writing or whatever it was. Everybody wanted a medal, but I knew I'd never get one because I wasn't the best in anything. And at the end of school, you know what happened?"

"What?"

"She called my name. The others all thought it was a joke. But she wasn't laughing. She said, 'Al wins a medal for building the best fires.'"

"And it *wasn't* a joke?" asked Sarah Ida.

"No. She gave me the medal. One of the big boys said, 'You better keep that, Al, because it's the only one you'll ever get.'"

"And did you keep it?"

He held up his watch chain. Something was hanging from it—something that looked like a worn, old coin.

"That's what you won?" asked Sarah Ida. He nodded.

"That's a medal?" she said. "That little old piece of tin?"

She shouldn't have said it. As soon as the words were out, she was sorry.

54

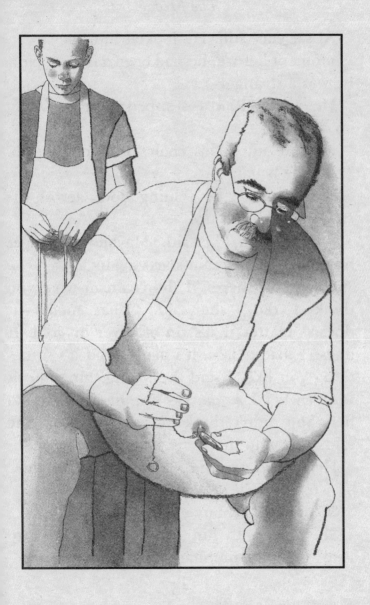

Al sat very still. He looked into the street. A moment before, he had been a friend. Now he was a stranger.

He said, "Rain's stopped. For a while, anyway."

He slid out of his chair. She got up, too. "I—" she began.

He dragged the folding door across the stand and locked up.

"Go on. Run," he said. "Maybe you can get home before the rain starts again."

She stood there. "I didn't mean what you think I did," she said. "That medal—it doesn't matter if it's tin or silver or gold. It doesn't matter *what* it's made of, if it's something you like. I said the wrong thing, but it wasn't what I *meant*. I—" He had his back to her. She didn't think he was listening. She said, "*Listen* to me!"

He turned around. "You like ice cream?"

"Yes," she said.

"Come on. I'll buy you a cone."

She went with him, around the corner to Pearl's Ice Cream Shack.

56

"What kind?" he asked.

"Chocolate," she said.

They sat on a bench inside the Shack and ate their chocolate cones.

"It's raining again," he said.

"Yes," she said.

Then they were quiet, while they listened to the rain. And she was happy because the stranger was gone and Al was back.

The Accident

For a month it went on that way—she and
Al working and talking together. She'd
thought it would go on and on like that.

Then came the day of the accident.

Al had run out of black shoe polish. He
told her, "I'll go over to the store and pick up
some more."

"I'll go," she said.

"No," he said. "You keep on with what
you're doing."

She finished with her customer. By that time
Al was coming back across the street. He
hardly ever walked. He almost always ran.
He was running now, with his head down.

58

The Accident

He was nearly to the curb, when a long, blue car came around the corner.

She shouted. She was too late. The car struck him. He spun around and fell, half on the sidewalk, half on the street.

The car stopped. A man jumped out. His face was pale. "He walked right in front of me," he said. "I couldn't stop."

Other people came running.

"Don't try to move him," someone said. "Wait for the ambulance."

The ambulance came screaming down Grand Avenue. It stopped near the stand.

Sarah Ida pushed through the crowd. She saw Al lying across the curb. He looked like a bundle of old clothes.

Two men in white were there. They turned him over. She saw his eyes looking up at her. He reached into his pocket.

One of the men said, "Don't move."

Something fell out of Al's hand and onto the sidewalk. She picked it up. It was the key to the shoeshine stand.

"Lock up," he said in a whisper, "and go on home."

The two men lifted him into the ambulance. The ambulance went screaming on down the street.

The crowds moved away. Sarah Ida was alone. She felt numb. She went over to the stand and sat down.

On the sidewalk was the can of shoe polish Al had bought. She sat looking at it.

Someone spoke to her. It was a man she knew — a customer. "Where's Al?"

"He's . . . gone," she said.

"Well, can you give me a shine?"

He climbed into a chair. She could hardly think, but her hands knew what to do. She shined his shoes.

Another customer came by. She shined *his* shoes.

Then a tall young man was there. She had never seen him before. "I'm from the newspaper," he said. "Did you see the accident?"

She nodded.

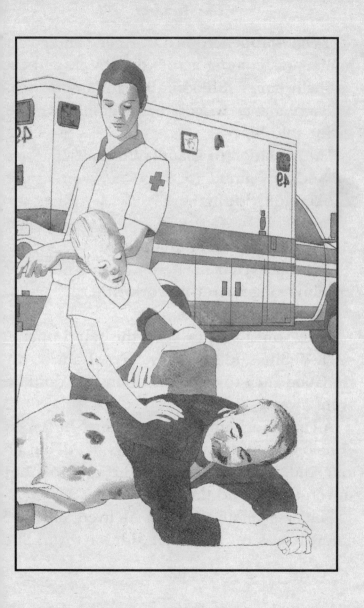

"What happened?"

"He was coming across the street, and the car — the car —" She couldn't go on.

"What's your name?" he asked.

She told him.

"Any relation to Claudia Becker?"

"She's my aunt."

"Are you visiting her?"

"Yes."

"How old are you? About ten?"

"Nearer eleven."

"How long have you worked here?"

"A month."

"Are you going to keep the stand open?"

"I —" She said suddenly, "Yes, I am."

"Good luck to you," the man said, and he went away.

A customer came, then another. She hoped someone would bring her news of Al, but no one did. Late in the day she took off her apron and closed the stand.

She wasn't sure where Al lived, but she knew it was on the other side of town. She went down Grand Avenue and across the railroad tracks. She came to streets where the houses were small and close together.

She asked several people, "Do you know where Al Winkler lives?" At last she found someone who told her.

She found the house. It was tiny and it needed paint. A woman came to the door.

Sarah Ida asked, "Could I see Al?"

The woman had been crying. She said, "Al's not here. He's been hurt."

"Didn't the ambulance bring him home?" asked Sarah Ida.

"No. He's in the hospital," said the woman. "You must be Sarah Ida. I'm Doris. I'm Al's wife. Come on in."

Sarah Ida went into a small, neat room.

"I just came from the hospital," said the woman.

"How is he?" asked Sarah Ida.

"I don't know. They don't tell you anything." Tears ran down the woman's cheeks. "I don't know what we're going to do."

"I brought you this." Sarah Ida took the money out of her pocket and put it down on a chair. "It's what I made today. I kept out some change. I'll need that for tomorrow."

"Thanks," said the woman.

"I'll be over again. I hope Al is going to be all right."

Sarah Ida went home.

Aunt Claudia said, "Do you know what time it is? I've been waiting—" She saw Sarah Ida's face. "What is it?" she asked.

Sarah Ida told her what had happened. "I'm going to keep the stand open."

She waited for Aunt Claudia to say, "You can't keep it open all by yourself."

But Aunt Claudia said instead, "Yes. I think you should."

Across the
Railroad Tracks

Sarah Ida was up early in the morning.

"I just called the hospital," Aunt Claudia said. "The nurse said Al had a good night."

"They don't tell you anything," said Sarah Ida.

She could hardly eat her breakfast. There was a lump in her throat.

"Will you be home for lunch?" asked Aunt Claudia, as Sarah Ida left the house.

"I forgot about lunch. No, I won't have time," said Sarah Ida, and she hurried off to Shoeshine Corner.

She unlocked the folding door and pushed it back. It was strange being there without Al. She thought of the way he'd looked up at her and reached for the key. Even then he'd been thinking about the shoeshine stand.

It meant a lot to him. She was right to keep it open.

Every morning Al bought a newspaper for the customers to read. She ran up the street and bought a paper. She put it on one of the chairs in the stand.

Back in a corner she found Al's broom, and she swept the sidewalk in front of the stand. She didn't expect much business so early in the morning. People were on their way to work. They didn't have time to stop.

But this morning they kept looking at her as they went by. Some of them smiled. Some of them spoke to her.

She heard someone say, "There's the girl!"

A customer came. He was the man from the pet store up the street. He said, "That was a nice story about you."

"*What* was a nice story?" she asked.

"Haven't you seen it? It's right here." He showed her the paper. There on the front page she saw the words:

SHOESHINE GIRL
KEEPS STAND OPEN

There was a story about her and Al. It told how Al was struck by a car — how ten-year-old Sarah Ida Becker was keeping the stand open while Al was in the hospital.

"Is that why people are looking at me?" she asked.

"It probably is," said the man.

When she finished with his shoes, he gave her a five-dollar bill. "It's for Al," he told her. "He can use it."

Most of the morning she was busy. Almost every customer asked about Al and left money for him.

At noon she heard someone say, "Hello, Sarah Ida." When she looked up, Rossi Wigginhorn was there.

Rossi was smiling. "Your aunt was afraid

you'd get hungry," she said. "She sent you this."

She held out a paper bag. Sarah Ida looked into it. There was a sandwich. There was a carton of milk with a straw. There was an apple.

"I don't see how I can eat this," said Sarah Ida.

"Why not?" asked Rossi.

"Look." Sarah Ida held out her hands with shoe polish on them.

"You can drink the milk with the straw," said Rossi, "and I can feed you the rest."

She was laughing. Sarah Ida laughed a little, too. "I know what," she said. "I'll go to the filling station and wash my hands. Can you stay here a minute? If any customers come, tell them I'll be right back."

She washed her hands at the station. When she came back, a customer was waiting.

"Go ahead. Have your lunch," the man said. "I've got time."

She had her lunch.

Rossi was saying, "I read about you in the paper. Did you know you're famous?"

"No," said Sarah Ida.

"Well, you are. Everybody thinks it's wonderful the way you're running the stand all by yourself. I wish I could help."

Sarah Ida looked at Rossi's pink and white dress. "You'd get awfully dirty."

"I don't care," said Rossi.

"Your mother would care," said Sarah Ida. "And you've helped already. You brought my lunch."

"Shall I bring it tomorrow?"

"No. I'll bring something from home," said Sarah Ida. "Thanks, anyway."

By the time Rossi left, there was a customer in every chair. Sarah Ida was busy all afternoon. At the end of the day, her arms ached and there was a crick in her neck, but her apron pockets were stuffed with money. She took it out and put it into the pockets of her jeans.

She locked the stand and started down to

Al's. She saw a boy walking behind her, half a block away. She had a feeling he was following her, but when she looked again, he was gone.

She crossed the railroad tracks, and she saw the boy again. This time he was ahead of her. She wondered how he had got there so fast. He must have run down a side street.

He seemed to be waiting for her. Now she knew him. It was Kicker.

She came up to him. The sidewalk was narrow, and he was in the middle of it. She stopped.

"What do you think you're doing here?" he asked.

"I'm going to Al's," she said.

"Al's not home. You ought to know that."

"I'm going to see his wife."

"What for?"

"Business," she said.

"What business?"

"*My* business," she said.

"You bringing money?"

71

"I don't have to tell you."

"You *are* bringing money. I see it in your pockets," said Kicker. "You better get out of here."

"Do you own this end of town?"

"There's something I could tell you about it. Listen. There's a gang here. If they think you've got money, they'll get it away from you."

"I was here yesterday. I didn't see any gang."

"You were lucky."

"Get out of my way," she said. "I'm going to Al's."

"All right." He stepped aside. "Go on, you fool."

She went past him.

"But if you're going to be a fool," he said, "I'm going with you."

He walked behind her all the way to Al's house. She knocked at the door. No one answered.

She turned back toward home.

Still Kicker walked behind her. He followed her to the railroad tracks.

"You were lucky again," he said. "But don't you ever come down here with money any more."

She walked on alone. She was thinking. Kicker was ugly. He was mean. She'd hated him for trying to bully her.

And now she didn't hate him. Because maybe there *had* been danger and he'd been trying to help her. Maybe she *had* been a fool because she hadn't listened.

A Letter

That night she and Aunt Claudia went to the hospital. They found Al in a room with two other men. He was sleeping.

His wife was sitting by the bed.

"I went to your house today," Sarah Ida told her.

"I wasn't home," said Doris. "I've been here with Al."

"How is he?" asked Aunt Claudia.

"Better," said Doris. "At first they thought he was — you know — hurt inside. But they found out he wasn't. They think he can go home tomorrow."

Al woke up. He saw Aunt Claudia first.

74

"Miss Becker!" he said. "I couldn't believe it was you."

She shook his hand.

Sarah Ida went to the bed.

"I guess I'll talk to you," he said, "even if you didn't do what I told you."

"What was it I didn't do?"

"The other day I told you to lock up and go home," he said. "You didn't do it."

"Aren't you glad I didn't? Look." She began to take money out of her pockets and spread it out on the bed.

He picked up some of the money. He turned it over in his hand. "Where did you get this?"

"Customers."

"You didn't *ask* for this, did you?"

"I didn't ask for anything," she said.

"They like you, Al," said his wife.

"But it's not mine," he said. "Some of it goes to Sarah Ida."

"No," she said.

"We'll see about it," he said. "When I'm back on my feet, we'll see about it."

"When will you be back on your feet?" asked Aunt Claudia.

"Well, I got a bad place here." He put a hand to his ribs. "But I'll be back at work sooner than you think."

* * *

Al was back at work in a week. He and Sarah Ida were working side by side again. Old friends and customers were stopping to talk.

"We didn't get much done," Sarah Ida said to Aunt Claudia that evening. "It was like a party. Everybody was glad to see Al."

"How is he?" asked Aunt Claudia.

"Not quite as quick as he was," said Sarah Ida. "I know his side hurts sometimes. But he's all right, with me to help him."

They had finished dinner and were sitting at the table. Sarah Ida looked at the clock. "Rossi is coming over. Shall we do the dishes now, before she gets here?"

"I'll do them later," said Aunt Claudia. "I want to talk to you—about a letter I had today."

76

"From my mother?" asked Sarah Ida.

"From your father. He wants you to come home."

"I'm not going," said Sarah Ida.

"It's not long till school starts," said Aunt Claudia. "You'll be going then, anyway."

"I can go to school here," said Sarah Ida, "and after school and on weekends I can help Al."

"Your mother and father haven't been writing you all that happened at home," said Aunt Claudia. "They didn't want to worry you. But they need you."

"They never needed me before."

"That isn't true. And they need you more now. Your mother is ill. She's going to have to be away for a while—maybe a long time. She'll be in a hospital not far from home. You can see her every day. She and your father want you with them."

"Did they say that?" asked Sarah Ida.

"Yes. At a time like this they think the family should be together. And you can make things easier for them. In a way, you'll be making a home for your father. When you first came here, I'd have said you wouldn't be able to do it. Now I think you can."

Rossi came. She had brought a big cardboard box. "I got a kit," she said. "It's to make a lampshade. It looks like colored glass, only it isn't really. I thought we could put it together."

They went up to Sarah Ida's room. They sat on the floor and spread the pieces of colored plastic out on newspapers.

"Isn't this fun?" said Rossi, as they cut and glued.

"Yes," said Sarah Ida.

"You're awfully quiet," said Rossi.

"I'm thinking," said Sarah Ida.

They finished the lampshade. Rossi held it up and let the light shine through it. "Isn't it pretty? It would look good here. Why don't I give it to you, and you can put it on that little lamp?"

"No, it's yours," said Sarah Ida. "Anyway, I may not be here much longer."

The Package

She and Al talked about it. After work the next afternoon they had chocolate cones at Pearl's Ice Cream Shack, and she told him about her father's letter.

"I have to go, don't I?" she said.

"Looks like it," he said. "Maybe you don't want to, but if you do go, you'll feel better in after years."

It made her feel sad to hear him say "in after years." She said, "You never know what's going to happen, do you?"

"That's right. You never know. All you can do is try to be ready for whatever does happen."

"What if I go on Monday? That way I could help you through the weekend."

"Monday would be fine."

"I hate to leave when you're just out of the hospital —"

"I'll get along."

"Maybe you can find someone to help you. Someone like Kicker."

"Maybe. I think he'd like to work for me now. He saw what a good thing you made of it. But I'm in no hurry to find anyone."

There was something she had to ask, even though she did feel foolish. "That apron you got for me to wear— Could I—could I have it?"

"It's a dirty old apron now. What do you want it for?"

"I just want it."

He didn't say yes or no, but after her last day at Shoeshine Corner, he said, "Roll up your apron and take it with you, if you want it."

* * *

The Package

On Monday morning Sarah Ida packed her things, and Aunt Claudia took her to the station. Rossi came along in the taxi. "You'll be riding all day," she said. "I made you some cupcakes so you won't get hungry."

They waited for the train. All at once, Sarah Ida looked up, and Al was there!

"Why aren't you at the stand?" she asked. "You'll miss a lot of customers."

He looked a little embarrassed. "I just thought I'd take a few minutes to see you off."

The train came in.

Aunt Claudia and Rossi said good-by. Al said, "You get on, and I'll help you with your things."

He handed up her suitcase. He had a little package wrapped in brown paper, and he slipped it into her hand.

She found a seat by a window. She looked out and saw the three of them on the platform — Rossi, Aunt Claudia, and Al. They were waving. She waved back, and they were gone, and Palmville was gone.

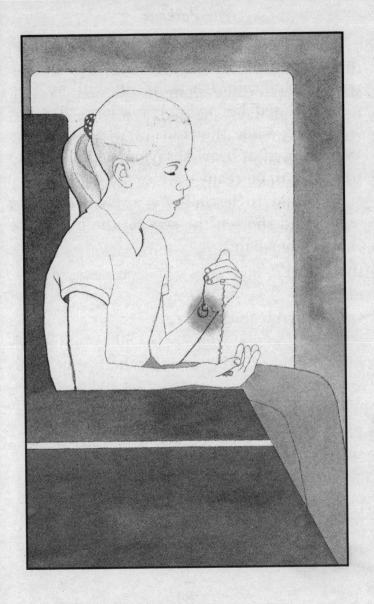

The Package

She opened the little package Al had given her. Inside was something that looked like an old, dull coin. It was Al's medal.

She closed her eyes. For a long time she sat there, while the train carried her along. She seemed to hear Al saying, "The thing to do is try to be ready—"

She said to herself, *I'm ready. I think I'm ready,* and she felt the star on the medal she held in her hand.

Also by Clyde Robert Bulla . . .

Pb 0-06-440333-5

A Lion to Guard Us
Left alone in seventeenth-century London, Amanda and her younger brother and sister must draw on their own resources to stay together and journey to America to find their father.

The Sword in the Tree
Young Shan dreams of becoming a great swordsman, just like his father, Lord Weldon. But Shan's world is shattered when his evil uncle surfaces with a plan to take over the family castle!

Pb 0-06-442132-5

Pb 0-06-443626-8

The Story of Valentine's Day
Valentine's Day wasn't always a time for candy and cards. This book traces the history of the holiday and its traditions over more than 2,000 years. Includes games, recipes, and crafts.

HarperTrophy®
An Imprint of HarperCollins*Publishers*

www.harperchildrens.com